P9-DFH-808

I Love
My Mom

For Olive, Joseph and Sam, with love.

SIMON & SCHUSTER BOOKS FOR YOUNG READERS
An imprint of Simon & Schuster Children's Publishing Division
1230 Avenue of the Americas, New York, New York 10020

First published in Australia in 2009 by Scholastic Press
Published by arrangement with Scholastic Australia Pty Limited
First U.S. edition 2010

For information about special discounts for bulk purchases, please contact
Simon & Schuster Special Sales at 1-866-506-1949 or
business@simonandschuster.com.
The Simon & Schuster Speakers Bureau can bring authors to your live event.
For more information or to book an event,
contact the Simon & Schuster Speakers Bureau at
1-866-248-3049 or visit our website at www.simonspeakers.com.
The text for this book is handwritten by Anna Walker.
The illustrations for this book are rendered in ink on watercolor paper.
Manufactured in Singapore
10 9 8 7 6 5 4 3 2 1
CIP data for this book is available from the Library of Congress.
ISBN 978-1-4169-8318-7

by Anna Walker

SIMON & SCHUSTER BOOKS FOR YOUNG READERS
New York • London • Toronto • Sydney

My name is Ollie.

I love my mom.

When I say, "Mom, what will we do?"

Mom says, "Let's try something new!"

We look

and talk,

we giggle

and walk.

We see a duck and a dragonfly.

We see orange fish
swimming by.

We love to play

with the butterflies.

We love to hide in disguise.

At home we rest
our tired feet
and Mom gives me
a special treat.

Mom says, "Is that a fish I see?"

"No, Mom, it's me, Ollie B."

But what I love best
is my kiss good night.
I love my mom.
Sweet dreams, night night.